I0579853

My Bodyguard

Celine Kyle

Copyright © 2024 by Celine Kyle

All rights reserved.

No portion of this book may be reproduced in any form without written permission from the publisher or author, except as permitted by U.S. copyright law.

Contents

Chapter 1

(Arabelle as Scarlett Rose Leithold, picture above)

'Hm' sighing I sat at the dining table, between Michael and Isaac. I looked at the food in front of me and started poking the aubergine. I don't even like aubergines, they're so squishy and just.... bah. I pushed the aubergine to the side of the plate and ate the rice instead. I loved rice, especially with sugar, but I like anything with sugar. I heard sugar is a drug, if that's true, I will call myself a drug addict from now on.

While enjoying my food I started observing Isaac who stared at the wall behind the table.

"Isaac, do you like aubergines?" I asked him. I know, odd question but I was so bored and wanted to start a conversation.

I patiently waited for an answer but never received one. He just looked at me for a second before focusing on the wall again. It was a try.

After finishing my food I stood up, grabbed my plate , my cutlery and made my way to the kitchen. I put everything into the dishwasher and went to my room, with Michael and Isaac following my every step.

I threw myself onto my bed and waited for Michael to close my door.

Michael was the oldest bodyguard in the house, he is 38 years old and 6'2 tall, the others are around 25 and about the same height or taller. One could think that Michael lacked in strenght or speed, but whoever thought that, was wrong. He worked out a lot in the training room, which was especially made for the bodyguards. He had more experience than the others and was the second best fighter in the whole house. He started working for my brothers about 5 years ago, so i've known him since I was 12. But he never really talked to me.

Actually no one here really talks to me, not that I am angry at them for not talking to me, I mean they must have their reasons. Sometimes when I get really bored I go to the room next to the bodyguard's lounge and listen to their conversations through the wall. I don't know why, but it calms me down whenever I am upset.

Suddenly my door opened and the loud bang noise interrupted my thoughts. Isaac and Michael positioned themselves in front of me and immediatly relaxed when they saw it was Xander.

"Stand up Arabella." I guess I missed someone out when I said no one talks to me, because Xander does, but not in a friendly way.

I slowly stood up, I was confused. What did he want? Could I maybe ask him if we could go to the garden? The strongest fighter always has to accompany me whenever I wanted to go outside. If things were a little easier, I would go outside everyday. I love hearing the birds chirp and looking at the flowers. But Xander just won't allow me to go outside more often, he doesn't even give me an explanation, but I'm ok with it. It's his job, he would know what's best for me.

Again deep in my thoughts, I didn't notice that Xander snapped his fingers in front of my face.

"Look at me Arabella" He said in a stern voice and I looked up.

"Hello Xander" I greeted him in a cheery voice and gently smiled at him. He just glared at me and gave Isaac and Michael a sign to get out.

"Your brothers are coming tomorrow and are staying for 3 days, you are not allowed to distract them from their work and don't bother them with your presence." He spat in my face harshly, I ignored his tone and a huge grin made it's way to my face. My brothers are coming home,yay!

"Thanks for the information Xander, do you think I can go out and buy myself a nice dress befor they arrive?" I asked him, waiting for his answer. I never asked him If we can go shopping before, this is the very first time. I never really asked him anything, except if we can go to the garden. I have to admit that I'm a little scared of Xander, he was so tall and strong and his eyes are so strict and hard.

"Okay, if you are not ready in 5 minutes you won't see the outside for the next 5 weeks." He said and left my room.

I threw on a pastel summer dress ,grapped my heart shaped purse and put a flower crown into my hair. Maybe I overdressed a little, but as I mentioned before, I barely get out and I wanted to look pretty for this special occasion.

I checked myself in the mirror and contently smiled at myself. I then put on my ballerinas as fast as I could and ran down the stairs.

I spotted Xander in the hallway and smiled at him. He looked at my outfit and grunted.

"Couldn't have been uglier." He said, but I tried to ignore it. It hurt, but maybe he had a bad day and now he has to accompany a 17 years old girl to a shopping tour, I wouldn't like that either if I were in his position. The more I thought about it, the guiltier I felt. But i quickly shook the guilt off,

I was too selfish right now, i still needed a new dress, because I didn't want my brothers to be ashamed of their younger sister.

A couple more bodyguards accompanied us to the mall, so we were 8 in total.

When the 3 black S.U.V.s pulled up to the car park and found a nice spot, we got out of the car. I squealed in happiness when I saw the big shopping paradise in front of me. Like every other girl my age, I loved shopping and couldn't wait to get in. When Xander saw me sqealing he just grunted at my childish behaviour and I instantly felt bad, the others didn't even pay attention.

I shook off the bad feeling and walked towards the big entrance. I won't let anyone ruin my mood, not like that's even possible, because I'm always happy :D

We entered and I stared at all the people in awe. There were girls and boys my age hanging out with their friends, young moms who had to take care of their young children, the elderly who just sat there and watched people go by and then there was us. 7 muscular tall men and one rather short girl, that must have been a funny sight.

I cheerfully walked in front of the guys, but was pulled back by Xander who painfully grabbed my wrist and I winced from the pain which flushed through my body, he looked me dead in the eye and growled "You will stay in the back Arabella." Spitting my name out like it was some kind of desease and then he let my wrist go. I held my wrist up to check whether there were any kind of bruises and saw that it was extremely red. I touched it but instantly pulled my finger back because of the pain. I sighed, angry at myself that I made Xander mad. I should have stayed in the back from the beginning.

Because I was too scared to ask Xander if we can go to Zara, I decided to ask James who walked right beside me instead. His face hold a stern and cold expression and I wasn't sure wether I should really ask him or just let it be. I decided to just go for it and ask him ,he actually seems like a nice person, at least when he wasn't on shift. I poked his arm with my right index finger.

"Uh J-j-jack could you please ask Xander whether we can go to Zara?"

He just stared at me like I was some kind of unicorn, he was surprised. But then his expression quickly changed in to an angry one.

"I'm not your fucking babysitter, ask him yourself for fucking god's sake." I cringed at hearing him cuss.

I figured that I would not be going to Zara today if I weren't to bring myself up to ask Xander. He would be even angrier if I would'n buy anything at all, because he would label our shopping trip as a waste of time and get mad at me again. I walked up to him, careful not to touch him or any of the men and cleared my throat to make him notice me.

"Um Xander could we maybe go to Zara? We can go home directly afterwards, but please." I pleaded and did the best puppy face I could do.

"We go to Zara and then we go home, and stop with that stupid look, it makes you just uglier." He said, my heart hurt a little at his words, but my head just ignored my heart. It's not that I like him, I guess it just hurts to be talked to so harshly.

"Ok" I said with my usual cheerful voice and smiled brightly.

We quickly went to Zara and a beautiful dark blue dress caught my attention. Dark blue is my brother's favourite colour.

Chapter 2

After we left Zara yesterday we directly went home, just as promised.

I bought the blue dress and I couldn't wait for my brothers to arrive this noon.

I haven't seen them in a year and I miss them dearly. I don't even have a phone which I could use to contact them, they wouldn't allow me to get one. I had a laptop, but many websites were banned and I would only use it to watch films and such anyways .

I looked at the clock and started to get ready, I wanted to look really good today. Maybe just today Xander wouldn't call me ugly, maybe just today.

I showered and shaved, I put on a mask to moisturize my skin and I put a little bit of make up on. Usually I don' t wear make up, but as I mentioned before, today was special. I still kept it natural.

I then put the dress on my bed, I didn't even get to try it on since Xander rushed me to buy it so we could get home. Now that I looked at it in a calmer atmosphere I didn't know if this dress wasn't too beautiful for someone like me. I'm not ugly, but this dress is just really pretty and I don't want to put shame on to it.

Ugh JUST WEAR IT, STOP WITH THE THINKING ARABELLE. I screamed at myself, I should stop worrying about things and just enjoy life. And that's what I'm going to do today, I'm going to enjoy my time with my brothers and I'm going to wear this dress, not wasting a thought on whether it suited me or not.

After I was finished getting ready, I made my way downstairs and walked right into the living room. I wonder where Isaac and Michael are, since they are in shift this whole week, but they will be around for sure.

I sat on the couch in the living room and waited for my brothers to come home.

When I heard the doors being opened I knew they had arrived, I ran towards the front door and saw my three brothers walk in.

Tyson, the youngest of them was the first to see me. He smiled at me and hugged me, he treated me the nicest, but I loved them all equally.

Then it was Alex' turn to hug me, he is the second oldest and just turned 26. I still remember how we used to play scrabble with each other and I would always win because he let me haha.

I then looked at my oldest brother, he just stood there in all his pride staring at me. I opend my arms wide, signalling him to hug me, but nothing happpened. He narrowed his eyes and stormed out of the hallway. I just stood there and tried to realise what just happened. Did I do something wrong? Did I anger him in any way? I looked wide eyed at my brother Tyson who just looked at the floor.

"Did I do something wrong Tyson?" I asked, unsure if I had the right to ask that question. I knew that Derek is strict, how couldn't I? I'm his sister, but did I do anything wrong?

"Don't worry about him princess, he just had a bad week, that's all" He told me and looked me in the eyes. I just nodded.

Alex left the hallway and went to the living room, Tyson and I followed him.

We all said down on the couch, talking about random stuff. After a couple of hours I decided to get something to eat and wanted to go the kitchen when I bumped into Xander. He growled lowly and pushed me out of the way and I fell against the cupboard. I groaned in pain and stood up shakily, holding my side. Xander just looked at me and then walked towards the living room.

I didn't have the time to treat my wound, since everyone in the living room was hungry and i volunteered to cook something.

I decided on Derek's favourite meal to lighten up his mood a little.

An hour passed and everything was ready, I took the mushrooms and put them on the dining table, I then did the same with the pork roast and I also prepared some salad.

Michael,Isaac,Xander my brothers and I sat on the table and shoved food onto our plates. It was dead silent while we ate.

Then Alex spoke up "This is really good Belle, thanks for the afford lil' sis"

I smiled at him and thanked him for the compliment "But you don't have to thank me Alex, today's a special day so this was necessary to celebrate you coming home, you're my brothers after all." I explained while smiling even brighter. From the corner of my eye I saw that Derek clenched his fist.

"Derek what is wrong?" I asked, worrying about him.

"I'm going to see you in our office in 20 minutes Arabelle"

I just sat there shaking a little, whenever he wants me to come to his office something bad had happened.

He then stood up and left the table.

I looked at my plate, suddenly feeling full. I went to the kitchen and cleaned up my plate. I excused myself and then went upstairs to my room.

After a while I walked towards his office , already preparing myself for the worst. I knocked on the door, then saw Xander open it. He stared down at me, I flinched a little, focusing on the floor underneath my feet. Has the floor always been this interesting?

I almost stumbled over my own feet while I entered the office because I was so nervous. What did I do wrong? Why would he want me to come to his office? I'm never allowed here unless he wants me to be here.

I looked up to see my brother staring at me, no emotion in his eyes.

"We will have to increase the amount of bodyguards, Xander wil be around you 24/7 from now on. I hope that you'll begin to understand that this world is a dark place and someone like you has to be protected at all times. As you know we have many enemies and I don't want you to get hurt, I hope you understand that."

I just nodded. It felt good, knowing that your brother cares for you. I already wondered what had done wrong, but if it's just about security, I'm ok with it.

One thing which worried me a little, is that Xander will be around me more often from now on. I should be relieved that there will be someone around me , who is actually willing to talk to me, but I wasn't.

Chapter 3

(Michael Fassbender starring as Michael Wolf, picture above)

I cuddled into my pillows, sighing contently. I adore pillows, doesn't matter what shape, what size, what colour, as long as they're comfortable, I don't care.

"What the fuck are you doing there?" Xander asks me while I push my cute pillows behind me, protecting them from him.

"I'm just cuddling with my pillows." I say and pout a little, why does he have to be so freaking mean all the time.

"Yeah, keep cuddling your pillows, that's probably the only thing in life you'll ever cuddle." He says smirking to himself. I just look down, he's kind of right even though I hate to admit it.

I never had a boyfriend, well how can I speak of a boyfriend when I never even had friends? People here don't really like me and as you know I don't get out tooo much. Maybe I just have to try harder, I can't stay friendless forever right? I could just cook for everyone, we have enough ingredients so there should be no problem. And my mother once said 'The best way to a man's heart is through his stomach'.

So I stood up, put on some cute unicorn slippers and went downstairs to the kitchen. Xander looked at me confused but followed in silence.

I opened the fridge and put everything I needed on the dining table beside me. I took the eggs out of their package, cracked them into a bowl , added milk, flour, sugar, vanilla extract and some baking powder. I mixed everything together until the ingredients combined well and sprayed cooking oil into a pan, I then started to pour a bit of the pancake dough into the pan and waited until the pancake was ready to be turned.

I piled the pancakes on 4 huge plates. I asked Xander whether he could help me, but he just ignored me. I shrugged and took one of the plates to carry it to the bodyguards lounge.

I knocked a few times, when James opened the door. He looked at me in anger, but then noticed the pancakes in my hands. His eyes brightend up a little and he opened the door for me so I could step in. I saw everyone sitting on a huge couch, playing a video game or something like that, laughing and enjoying their time. James cleared his throat and everyone turned their heads in our direction, staring at me wide-eyed.

"What is she doing here??" One of them, I think his name is Jackson, asked.

"Uh I-I have pancakes." I replied shyly even though i knew that the question wasn't directed at me.

Everyone looked at me, then at the pancakes. I almost dropped them, since they started getting really heavy and I barely worked out. I handed them to James who still was beside me and he happily took them out of my hands. One of the younger Bodyguards offered me a seat and I thankfully sat down. Suddenly Xander grabbed my arm and yanked me away from the couch. He lowered his hands from my arm to my wrist and held me by my wrist tightly just like he did in the mall. I groaned out in pain trying to push his hands off, he only tightend his grip on my already bruised wrist.

The pained look on my face must have alarmed the guy who offered me a seat earlier. He pushed Xander back , Xander loosend his grip and I instantly yanked my wrist back and hold it against my chest, protecting it from any further abuse.

Xander glared at me and slowly approached me, I ,on the other hand stepped back until I felt the wall hit my back. Fear blinded my senses and I couldn't see anything but the angry look on Xander's face.

I didn't even notice how Michael and Isaac stepped beside me.

"Stop Xander,you're scaring her." Michael said in a voice which one wouldn't dare to object.

Xander growled lowly and stormed out of the room.

Isaac handed me a cool pack and I thankfully looked him in the eyes a smile plastered on my face.

"Now get out Arabelle." Michael said in a calm but stern voice. My smile instantly dropped.

"B-b-b-ut X-x-ander ist g-g-oing to h-h-urt me if I g-go back." I stuttered, shocked at the fact that they are sending me back . The fear of getting hurt by Xander controlled my mind and mouth.

Instead of answering, Michael pushed me out of the door. I looked down the long corridor, seeing Xander standing in front of the stairs, which lead up to my room. In order to avoid him, I quickly walked the other way. I tip toed towards the kitchen, when I was gripped from behind.

"Where the fuck do you think are you going?!" Xander shouted angrily at me.

I slowly turned around, looking down to the floor.

"I uh, I-I wanted to get a s-sandwich" I told him weakly, still not looking into his eyes.

He groaned in response, like he always does. He then stepped in front of me , stepping into the kitchen and walking towards the counter, pulling bread and cheese out of the fridge.

"What? Are you just going to stare at me or are you going to help me make your damn sandwhich?"

"That's not how you speak to my little sister Xander" A familiar voice interupted Xander's and my conversation. I turned around, to get a better look at the person who was talking to us. My brother.

I havn' t heard his voice in long time, making it sound almost foreign to me.

"Derek?", I asked confused. "Why are you here?"

"I was looking for my baby sister, do you have a problem with that Belle?"

"No not at all, but why were you looking for me?" I tilted my head to the side, looking up to him with a confused expression on my face. "Wasn't he angry at me just a few hours ago?" I asked out loud by accident.

"I wasn't angry at you Arabelle, I was angry at something you shouldn't care about, ok baby girl? Now come on and hug your big bro." He gestured me to come and hug him and I gladly accepted the offer, you would too if you were in my position.

A few minutes passed by, my brother and I were still in the same position as before and Xander just awkwardly watched us.

"Eeeeeh, when exactly are you letting me go Bro?" I asked, wiggling in his tight hold.

"I'm never going to let you go. Someone will snatch you away from me if I do and big bro doesn't want that." Ok, why is he acting like this all of a sudden, I can't say that I didn't enjoy it, I mean I missed my brothers over the last year, but I'm not used to this behaviour, I would expect such a behaviour from Tyson or Alex, but not from big bad Derek. And what is he talking about, someone snatching me away from him? Not like that's going to happen, my brother doesn't have to worry about boyfriends.

"No one will snatch me away from you, look at me. Do I look like I will ever get a boyfriend?" I ask in all honesty.

Chapter 4

I calmly sat on my bed, watching my favourite movie.

"Damn that movie sucks."

"No it doesn't, it's just too cool and awesome for you." I replied, looking at the grumbling Xander who sat on a chair next to my bed.

"Well, that girl is just as ugly as you" Was his only comment on the movie. I turned around and stared at him, his brows furrowed .

"If you had a girlfriend, would you treat her like you treat me?" I asked bravely. I guess I just asked the only question which truly intrested me and I waited patiently for an answer. But it never came.

Instead my brother Tyson bursted through the door and screamed.

"THERE'S A FUCKING SPIDER N MY ROOM! GET RID OF IT BELLE!" I laughed at his command and slowly got up from my bed.His room is only a few meters away from mine , so the walk wasn't too long. However, as we arrived we saw Max already patiently waiting for us."What are you doing here Max? Your room is at the end of the hallway" I giggled.

"Arabelle this is not funny. What would you do if the spider were to crawl into my room? Huh? Got no answer, I knew it." Max replied.It was truly something you don't hear everyday.Two big and strong guys afraid of a small spider which wouldn't hurt anyone. I laughed even louder at that thought.

"STOP LAUGHING" Max and Tyson screamed at me in union.

I slipped into the room and looked for the spider."But I can t even see it, where is that spider Tyson?"

"R-right there, there is the m-monster" He stuttered and pointed behind the dustbin"

I looked at the small thing, crawling on the floor."You're really afraid of that teeny-tiny spider?"I just couldn't stop laughing, how could they ever think of a spider as a threat?

"What's going on in here?" Derreck , who just stepped into the room asked.I looked up at him, a smile still prominent on my lips.

"Oh nothing, just me getting rid of a spider because my brothers are to scared to do it"

"Are you fucking serious guys? A spider?"

"Sir, there is a visitor, he claimed it's important." Xander informed DerreckDerrick calmly stepped out of the room and went downstairs.I watched him and rushed after him, curious for the stranger.

As i reached the bottom of the stairs I bumped into something hard, I looked up to see Xander evilly glaring down at me.

"You're not supposed to be here Arabelle." He said clenching his teeth.

"Oh, who is this lady? Such a beauty. Is that your little sister Derreck?"

"Why are you here Evan?" Derreck growled at the man standing in the doorway.

"I originally wanted to remind you of our deal, but now that I've met your adorable little sister..."

"Don't you fucking dare, leave my sister out of this."

"Hahaha, is the big brother a little protective of his princess?"

I was totally and utterly scared, I hid behind Xander, who protectively stood in front of me."

"Get fucking lost Evan""Oh, is Xander a little mad at me? Come on princess, step forward so I can have a better look at you." The guy creepily said.

I pressed my face into Xander's chest, hiding my face from 'Evan'.Xander put his arms around me, shielding me from Evan's stares.

"She won't do such things." Xander darkly growled.

"Take her upstairs and stay with her." Derrick said to Xander. Xander lifted my legs up, I clung onto him while hiding my face in his chest.

He carried me to my room and caressed my hair while doing so.

"Shhh, it's ok"

He sat down on my bed, me being in his lap.

"W-who w-was that?" I asked him.

"No one you should be concerned about baby girl."

I looked at him with wide eyes, his eyes softened before turning hard again.

He threw me onto my bed and quickly left my room, leaving me cold.

I looked after him and then fell asleep.

Chapter 5

I woke up to the shouting which could be heard in the whole entire house."HE FUCKING WANTS HER" my brother Tyson yelled in anger"DON'T ACT LIKE I DON'T KNOW, DUMBASS" could be heard from Alex."Shut the fuck up, yelling at each other won't help. We need to get rid of him before he tries anything."

I , still insanely sleepy, crawled out of my bed, opened the door and made my way to my 3 brothers.

An expression of surprise covered my face, as I saw not only my brothers, but also Xander,Michael, James and a few others standing in the living room."Can I help you with something?" I asked shyly, not trying to anger them even more. Both, my ears and my heart, were incredible sensitive to screaming.

Instead of answering, Tyson pulled me towards him and hugged the living daylight out of me. Scared of being squished to death I looked at Derek pleadingly. He instantly moved to Tyson, slapped his head and pulled me out of my brother's embrace.

"Arabelle,.." Derek sighed."Did something happen while I was asleep?" I asked innocently, rubbing the sleep out of my eyes."No, nothing that you should worry your pretty little head about, alright? Soo, what does my favourite little sister want to do today?" I couldn't help but be a little suspicious, I blantly waved it off, probably nothing serious.

"Can we go to the zoo please?" I plead, pouting and giving my brother the best puppy dog eyes I could master.

"No!" Barked Xander. I hung my head lowly, already seeing all the elephants and penguins blurring until they were completely gone.

"Arabelle, you know that public places are too dangerous for an innocent soul like you. Let's rather stay here and watch a movie, alright?"

"But Alex, I'm at home watching movies every single day..." I pouted

I tried looking even sadder than I actually was, a crocodile tear fell down onto my cheek and I looked into Derek's eyes hopefully .

"Oh, god damn it" groaned Derek"Alright we're going to the zoo, but there will be a few rules. 1. Don't run off, you're always to be at either mine, Alex', Tyson's or Xander's side.2. If someone orders you to do something, you will do the task asked of you without a question. This is all for your safety baby sis.3. When we decide that we should leave, you won't compl ain."Derek said with a strict voice. I just beamed at him, too happy to even properly listen, I mean this is my very first time at the Zoo and I've only ever seen animals in films and shows.

"Alright we're going, Arabelle get your Jacket and a hat from upstairs, it's cold today. Xander,   Michael, James you and a few others will be coming with us, tell Jackson, Lukas, Tim and John to come as well." Derek ordered in his meany-voice.

The car ride was pretty silent.... I think?I was too focused on the images of the zoo in my head. Would they have bunnies? Or even a little baby goat? I hope they do...Suddenly a big rough hand shook me out of my thoughts and I turned around to see Xander.

"We're here" was all he said, or was all I heard, before I jumped out of the car and ran towards the entrance.

I got jerked back by the same rough hand, which shook me in the car already. "You never are to leave my side" He growled angrily,I just nodded my head while looking down at my feet.

I didn't even notice Tyson coming to my side, pulling my hand into his and dragging me to the nice looking lady who sold the tickets.

"Ok, here you go. 11 adult tickets to the park and the slide. Oh and btw, you are a beautiful couple" She said smiling, while I blushed."Oh, we are siblings" I quickly corrected her."Then who of the bunch is your boyfriend." She asked while winking at me." I don't have one" I whispered quietly while blushing like crazy, my eyes still looking down to my feet.

She slightly gasped "How is a beautiful little girl like you single? But if you want to, I have a son your age you could..." she got broken off by Xander"She will be fine, thank you." He growled out and pulled me into the Zoo.

"Hey! That was rude Xander!" I pouted at him, how can he be so disrespectful to someone obviously older than him. He just ignored me and pushed me to Lukas, I instantly recognised him as the younger man who helped me with Xander and who offered me a seat."Hello, I'm Arabelle" I greeted him cheerily and stuck my hand out, for him to shake it.

Unlike my expectations, he also reached his hand out for me to shake and gave me a wide friendly smile.My heart lightly swelled at the possibility of making a friend, who would finally talk to me, or even like me..."So Lukas, what is your favourite thing in the world?" I asked him, smiling the whole time.

"Hm" he thought, "I'm not sure, I'd probably have to say my family and right after that, maybe your smile" He said winking at me, which resulted in me being a blushing mess.

A hand suddenly grabbed me from behind and pushed me behind a huge back. Xander

"Stop fucking flirting around Lukas and focus on your damn job." He gritted out. I flinched slightly as I heard him cussing, I just really don't like it. How do those bad words actually help in our daily vocabulary? They are completely and utterly useless.

"Hey Belle, look, do you see the monkeys tolling around over there?" Alex asked, pulling me out of my thoughts.The animals! How could I forgot watching all the animals!I quickly ran towards the fence which separated me from the small brown and furry creatures.They were so adorable. Jumping around from branch to branch.

A light laugh could be heard from behind me, I turned around to look at the person making fun of me, pouting a little while doing so.

"What did I do?" I asked Lukas."Oh nothing babe, you only looked so cute" he smiled. I, of course, blushed at his words and the nickname he gave me. Xander beside me just glared at Lukas.

Chapter 6

"You know what he said about you wasn't true?" Xander asked, he rather accused me."I know." I responded submissively, my head hanging low."He only wants to play you, fuck you, then leave you. He wouldn't actually like you." He stated."I know." A lonely tear slid down my cheek.He muttered something as I just sat on my bed.I knew all the things he said, I would have worded them differently, but I kind of knew that there would be something wrong when someone actually talked humanly to me.I guess I just didn't deserve friends. I can't think of anything I did, but I must have done something wrong for everyone to hate me.But hey, I still have my brothers.

Ok, stop all the negative thoughts Arabelle. Just sitting here doing nothing won't help you. Maybe Xander was wrong? I'm sure he was!

I jumped off my bed and ran down the stairs, I was met by Lukas who stood in the hallway, checking his phone. He gave me a warm smile as he recognised who I was.I ran over to him and hugged him, his arms wrapped themselves around me, squeezing me."Lukas? Can you help me please?" I asked him, giving him my best puppy dog eyes.

"What is it Babe? He asked smiling, his arms still around my waist.

"I uhm, I k-kind of want to make friends here and you know the others a lot better than I do. Can you help me make f-friends please?" I mumbled quietly, a stutter accompanied my words and I let my head hang , a bit embarrassed to openly admit that I was lonely, even if it was so obvious.

Lukas frowned a bit, thinking about what I had asked him.

"I'm not sure, it won't be as easy as you might think. I don't want you to get hurt by the others." "Oh I'm sure I'll be fine" I grinned at him, but my words obviously didn't give him any reassurance, as a frown was still plastered on his face.

"Well, I guess..." He mumbled.

I happily clapped my hands and ran towards the door, which separated me and the bodyguards.I knocked twice and quickly was faced with a grumpy looking Isaac.

"Hello Isaac, nice to see you again!" I threw him a blinding smile, in response He attempted to shut the door.However, key- word: attempted. He was stopped by Lukas foot, which was now stuck between the door and it's frame."Let her in Isaac" he sighed.Isaac, who was a little confused, opened the door wide enough for me to hush through. Unlike last time,there were barely any people in the room, I guess it just wasn't the time.I received a few stares, even glares as I made my way to the couch, where the majority of people sat and played on their PlayStation.Lukas sat beside me, wrapping his arms securely around my shoulders. After a while everyone stopped staring and continued their game.

Suddenly Michael entered the room. He looked surprised as he saw me sitting on the couch, I beamed at him as I saw his features soften a little.I jumped onto his arms, which he definitely didn't expect because be almost dropped me.

"What are you doing here?" He frowned and shot me light glare. He gently let me down as I still smiled at him, happy that he finally talked to me."I want to be your friend Michael!"He just pushed me to the side and and walked towards Lukas, who quietly watched us.

"Lukas I need to talk to you" was all I could hear, before the two big men left the room. I sat back onto the soft sofa and continued watching the guys play.

After a while I tapped Jackson's shoulder, he was too focused on the game. I tapped the boy sitting right next to me again. "Uhm, c-could I maybe a-also try playing?"He grunted, but stopped to look at me. Then he suddenly told the others to stop and handed me the controller.

"So the game's name is Fifa. It's easy, really. This is how you let them run, you need to press this button to shoot and here is how you turn and pass the ball to other players." I listened intently as he explained everything to me.

Then I started to play myself and boy was I good. I didn't need a lot of practice to kick the other guys' behinds, I was a natural haha.

A giggle left my mouth as I watched Louis, my opponent, look at the controller disbelievingly."What age did you start playing?"He asked me"Today" I answered, giggling even more.

A loud bang stopped my laughter and I looked at the intruder.

Xander roughly grabbed my hand and pulled me towards the door.Clumsy as I am, stumbled and my head hit the sharp edge of the couch table before dropping to the floor.

I gasped at the pain and I felt something liquidy as I laid there. Everyone stood around me, but I couldn't recognise any faces at the moment.My vision became blurry and and whimper left my mouth before I fell into the darkness.

Chapter 7

X ander All I saw was red when I saw her next to that little fucker, playing with him. As innocent as she was, she was completely oblivious to the looks other guys gave her. I hate taking her out just because I hated having to fend off a different little fucker who thought he could look at what was mine. Fucking mine and now here we are, some idiot invited her to the lounge, full of newcomers who could barely keep their dicks in their pants. Oh how wonderful.I grabbed her hand, a little too roughly and pulled her towards the door.Of course the little idiot fell and now here we are.At the fucking clinic.Derek is already going all ape-shit on me for letting something happen to his sister, so were the other two.

Instead of listening to what they were saying I watched the girl in front of me.Her blonde hair looked messy and bloody, she was pretty nonetheless.

I'm not stupid, I'm the cause of her painfully low self esteem. Of course I've seen the look she gives herself in the mirror, frowning whenever someone dares to make her a compliment, if anyone does so at all.

I couldn't decide whether I deeply hated or adored her.

"Fucking get your shit together and don't let your stupid anger out on Arabelle!" Screamed Derek at me. I rolled my eyes in response."Don't think I'm stupid Xander. I've seen the bruises on her wrist." Said Tyson in a deathly voice.I instantly felt bad.There's a difference between verbally and physically abusing someone. I never meant to really physically hurt her, I just couldn't control myself sometimes."I know, Tyson" was all I could say."The only reason we're keeping you is because you're our friend Xander, but if you continue hurting our little angel, we will have to beat you the fuck up."

The brothers left me and Arabelle alone, told me to guard her, I knew this will be a long fucking night.I tried getting comfortable on the chair in the corner in the room, but her trembling form stopped me.A few tears slid down her lovely cheeks and she started trashing around.The sight pained my heart, I hated her, but somehow seeing her this vulnerable was an unbearable sight for me to see. I pinned her arms down, to stop her from trashing around and possibly pulling the IVs out of her arms. She suddenly grabbed my arms and pulled me down to her. I wanted to stand up, but a whimper left her mouth as I tried to get her hands of me, so I stopped.Why was she so fucking weak. I hated weaklings, couldn't stand up for themselves for shit.I wanted her to yell at me whenever I pushed her away, but all she did was smile.She was way too innocent for the evil around her, she needed protection, but she would need to defend herself as well.Especially since Evan was after her now.Evan was the brothers' enemy.They tried cooperating a few weeks ago, but everything failed when he laid his eyes on her.

He wanted her, that was no secret. And if he had her, he would destroy her. But that's not going to happen. He'll need to step over my dead body first to get to her, and I don't die that easily.War would break out. The Mafia would try everything to get their little angel back.She was so naïve, so pure, she wasn't even aware of the fact that her brothers led the European Mafia.The Italians, the polish and the german made a pact, creating this extreme "Gang".And her brothers were the "Gangleaders". A word way too cheesy for what we were actually doing. Killing. Lots of killing.

So, it became my duty to protect Arabelle from all the evil going on around her.She is convinced that her brothers are working at some kind of bank and that she needs to be protected because of all the money the family owns, which is partly true.She won't need to know about the rest, it shouldn't be of her concern.

Chapter 8

I turned to the next page, deeply fascinated by the book I was reading at the moment.

Xander just sat on the chair in the corner of my room, he practically glared at the small display in his hands and looked like he wanted to shatter his phone at the next best opportunity.

"Did something happen, Xander?" I asked him tenderly.

"Mind your own fucking business." I immediatly stopped looking at him and instead, stared the floor down.

"I'm sorry" left my mouth as a whisper. I started focusing on my book again and quickly blended the grumpy cat in my room out.

I couldn't help but be a Little sad.My brothers left yesterday morning and left me alone with Xander and the others...My plan to make new friends crashed as well, not even Lukas would talk to me anymore.

I was all alone, once again.

"We need to go downstairs." Xander said grimly.

I quickly hopped of my bed and followed Xander out of my room down the stairs.

I saw Michael standing at the end of the staircase, looking at me worriedly.

"Is everything alright Michael?" I asked just as worried.

However, instead of answering me, he just turned around and walked away, not sparing me a second glance.

I looked down sadly.

Before my brothers left I thought something had changed, but once they left everything was back to normal.

Completely lost in my thoughts I didn't even notice how Xander suddenly stopped walking, resulting in me bumping into him harshly and falling onto the hardc marble steps.

"Oww", I groaned and looked up at the tall man who now turned towards me.

"You better be careful, or I will lock you in your room for the next few weeks." He growled at me.

I blushed out of embarrassment and looked down again.

"I'm sorry Xander"

We continued our way into the kitchen and I sat on one of the bar Hockers. In front of me stood Michael preparing breakfast for me.

"Michael can I please have pancakes today? Please, please, please!" I begged him desperately, cheering up a little at the thought of the delicious godness.

Michael didn't reply, but I know that he started preparing the dough.

"Thanks Michael!!" I thanked him gratefully. He just grunted as a response.

Xander just sat beside me, completely silent.

"Xander are you alright? You seem a little off today." I asked him innocently and worried.

"Shut up, I don't want to talk to you." He sneered at me.

Again I looked down, a little sad again.

My brothers leaving always got to me, the weeks after they leave are quite hard. It is indeed difficult to not be sad when the people who care for you just leave, without you knowing when you will see them again.

The delicious smell of pancakes pulled me out of my thoughts, I couldn't hold myself back and just started digging into to the huge pile of perfection.

I moaned loudly at the sweetness and all the heads in the room turned to me, my cheeks flushing with embarrassment I looked down to my lap and mumbled a quiet "sorry".

"Never do that again." Xander said darkly, seeming irritated by something.

I again mumbled a shy and quick "Sorry".

Michael broke the awkward silence in the room :" Xander, I need to talk to you. Right now."Both left the kitchen, Xander glancing over his shoulders , probably thinking about my brothers order to always be around me.

Actually enjoying the new found freedom I had without Xander constantly spreading his negativity, I skipped through the halls of the mansion. I stopped by the lounge the other guards had to be in and slowly opened the door.

I saw Lukas and James sitting on the sofa, playing Fifa and I made my way forward.

"Arabelle, what are you doing here? Where is Xander?" Lukas asked rushing his words.

"Michael took him away to talk. Would you mind if I watched you?" I asked shyly.

"Only if you sit there" James said, pointing at the other end of the room.

Appreciating that he actually led me stay, I walked to the corner on the opposite side of where they sat.

I sat down on the cold floor and watched them happily, I at least have something to do now.

I continued watching them happily and smiling, but the desire to play myself grew.

Lukas, who has been silent after the questions he asked me, kept glancing at me.

"Arabelle, do you maybe want to come play?" He asked.

Extremely happy I instantly shot up and sprinted to the couch.

"Yes please!!!!" I almost shouted, a huge grin spread across my face.

Lukas just chuckled at my behaviour.

I grabbed his controller, and just like the time before, beat James.

"I absolutely hate playing with you." James mumbled, now being in a bad mood.

I laughed loudly.

Lost in the play I didn't notice how the time flew by, until the door banged open, almost shattering against the wall.

Xander stood at the door step, shooting daggers at me. He looked angrier than ever before and it scared me to death .

I tried hiding behind James, trying to escape Xander's wrath.

"Where the fuck have you been?"He screamed in my face.

His screaming scared me even more, to the point where I was straight up trembling.

"In here?" I shyly answered , making it sound like a question

"Do you even fucking know that I have been looking everywhere for your stupid ass?" I cowered away from him as he insulted me and abused my poor ears with his screaming.

"I'm sorry" I whispered

"You are not sorry, oh no! You will just keep doing this shit, until they finally will get you! Arabelle, Evan is fucking dangerous! It would be easy for him to break into the house. But do you know what, maybe it's better for him to get you." He shouted angrily.

"What?" I looked up at him, tears building up behind my eyes.

"Your brothers are working so fucking much just to protect you, and you just wander around alone. Are you really such a selfish bitch, or is this just temporary?" He screamed again.

I started sobbing, whimpers coming out of my mouth.

Xander continued to grab my shoulders harshly, breathing hard.

A flash of guilt seemed to cross his features, but I must have imagined the empathetic emotion.

He dropped me and I curled up into a ball, still crying and sobbing.

He was right though, I didn't want to risk getting taken, I just selfishly roamed around the house, not waiting for Xander to come back.

The guilt started consuming me and just added to the emotional mess in my head, that started forming once my brothers left.

The crying and the overflowing emotions became to much for me and tired me, to the point where my eyes closed and I shut out my surroundings.

Chapter 9

Lukas The sight of small Arabelle lying on the floor with visible tear-streams on her cheeks was heart breaking. The crying must have tired her to the point, where she simply fell asleep right here.

I tried avoiding her, to avoid any emotional strings, but you just couldn't just leave this little lady alone, especially when she was as sad as she is now.

I made my way towards the small little angel, lying on the cold floor, wanting to pick her up and carry her to her bed, but someone beat me to it.

Xander.

He picked her up, his right arm supporting her back, his left arm under her knees.

I sneered at him angrily.

"What the fuck is your problem"

"The way you treat her is my problem, this can be counted as fucking abuse and especially this was just unnecessary. She was safe the entire fucking time." I whisper-shouted, careful to not wake her up.

"She is non of your damn business,Lukas." He said sternly.

"Oh, but she is yours?"

"I'm her first and personal guard, her safety is indeed my business." He coldly said.

"Does this include protecting her from yourself?" I asked in a provocative manner.

"I know that you just want to fuck her Lukas, don't pretend that you actually care for her" he snapped, loosing control over himself.

"You know shit, Black" I snapped, adressing him by his last name.

"Don't you dare feel things for her that you are not allowed to feel. She is fucking mine and she will always be fucking mine!" He responded, now full on screaming. Arabelle stirred a little, still not waking up, despite our fight.

"I will carry her up now, but if you dare look at her the wrong way, think about her inappropriately, or consider her as something more than just a job, I will rip you apart." He said coldly, fully controlled.

The two then left the lounge, the small girl still innocently lying in the beast's arms.

Fuck.

Fuck Xander.

He can go and suck my fucking cock, his little speech will not keep me away from her.

„You should listen to him Lukas" James suddenly said, pulling me out of my thoughts.

"Why, so he can continue fucking abusing her? Do you all hate her that much? What did she even ever fucking do to you?" I sneered at him angrily.

"Look, we do not hate her. She's as innocent as they get, in fact some of us feel things for her they probably shouldn't. But you see, Xander is a dangerous man and so are her brothers. Do you think they just would let it slide, if one of us came too close to her? He's a freak, he god damn owns her."

"What the fuck are you even saying? You are letting this poor girl suffer because you're scared?" I spat at him.

"You don't understand Lukas. Xander is as dangerous as the brothers themselves, if not even more so. He practically loves Arabelle, he just hasn't realised it yet."

"If that's the shit you call love I don't ever want to experience it." I ended the conversation and left the room.

Love. Of course.

Chapter 10

I woke up in my bed, not remembering how I got there after my little emotional outburst yesterday... embarrassing... and everyone there saw it too.... just embarrassing.

I felt my cheeks flushing with heat as I replayed yesterday's events, why did everything have to end up that way?

I sighed loudly as the door to my room opened and Xander steppend in.I crawled back a little, watching him from underneath my protecting blanket.

"I'm sorry." Was all he said as he watched me.

"What?" I whispered intimidated by his form.

"I'm sorry for the things that I said to you yesterday , it was uncalled for and therefore I apologise." He stated.

"Oh, uhm it's alright I g-guess?" I stuttered slightly and looked down to my lap.

"But Arabelle you also have to understand that it is dangerous for you to wander around by yourself. Even though this is your home, Evan is extremely powerful and he wants you. But believe me, as long as I'm there to protect you, nothing will happen to you." I looked up at him while he confidently spoke, I was actually quite moved by what he said, considering that nobody apart from my brothers actually said something so caring.

"Thank you Xander" I smiled at him brightly.

"What do you want to do today?" He asked, looking at me seeming genuinely interested.

"Ehm, can we...can we maybe go the park?" He looked annoyed.Oh no, I did it again. I made him angry once again.

"Arabelle, I just told you that even being here is dangerous. What makes you think that going to the park is safer?"

"I don't k-know, I...I just answered your question." I looked at my lap shyly, an awkward silence surrounded us, until he suddenly jumped up.

"Come on. I will ask Michael and the others to accompany us, Same rules as in the zoo though. I swear Arabelle, if you ever run off, I will chain you onto my arm." He said, looking into my eyes deeply.

I jumped up excitedly "Thank you Xander!!" I tried calming down a little to choose something to wear, which was almost impossible.

Xander left the room, I changed and then went after him. WE'RE GOING TO THE PARK!

-

The ride to the park was quiet, apart from my giggling of course.I couldn't have been happier, it's been years since I've been at the park!Suddenly the car came to a stop and I quickly jumped from my seat, too impatient to properly wait for the others to leave first.I was about to run to the flower field, as Xander pulled me back and threw me an angry glare.

The guards, like always, surround me, creating a bubble. Xander held my hand tightly, but not tight enough to actually hurt me.

"Can I go and collect some flowers, please?" I asked, Xander just looked down at me and nodded.

I almost ran to the flowers, to which Xander tightened his grip.

"Remember the rules, Arabelle."

Too distracted by the cute little daisies, I ignored his reminder."Can you hold these, please?" I looked at Xander expectingly, reaching my hand out to give him the flowers I collected, "they'd make a nice flower crown"

"Oh who do we have here?" Another man's voice destroyed our peaceful flower-moment.I tried looking at him but Xander blocked the view.

"Evan, what do you want?" Xander gritted our."Oh, you know what I want." Evan answered, sounding extremely creepy and perverted."Fucking get lost" I cringed at Xander's aggressive order. „Don't worry, I'll get her sooner or later anyways." Evan laughed evilly."Over my dead body and now get lost, before I shoot your and your guards' asses."

And then the only thing I heard was shooting.

"Bring her back to the car! Quickly!" Someone picked me up and quite literally covered my body with his own. He put me in my seat and ran to the driver's seat. The man, who I then recognised as Lukas, started the car and drove off.However, another pitch black car started following us, which led Lukas to speed up.

We arrived at the house after a few minutes only. I already saw multiple guards waiting for our car and when we arrived, they sprinted to my door, pulled me out and carried me into the house.

Isaac brought me to a room, I did not recognise, which was ironic, considering this was my own home.

"Listen Arabelle, under no circumstances will you leave this room, okay? You're gonna be fine, we're gonna be fine." He tried reassuring me. I just nodded, my eyes wide in shock and my mouth unable to mutter a single word.

And then, I was alone.

I really can't tell how many seconds, minutes or even hours passed.

The darkness, which penetrated the room, scared me. Not knowing what was going on scared me. Not knowing what happened to the others, to Xander or Lukas, scared me. The situation scared me.Tears started streaming down my face, when I suddenly heard a lock opening.

In relief I jumped towards the door, hoping for one of the guards to tell me it was all over.

"Oh little girl not so fast, not so fast" An evil voice whispered.He came inside the room and locked the door.Evan.I pushed myself to the corner and whimpered quietly.

"Oh baby, no need to cry. I'm not going to hurt you...maybe.' He laughed evilly.

I tried running to the other corner of the room, but he caught me in his arms.

"All I want is a little fun, before I get you permanently." He smirked and buried his face into my neck, while I trashed around.

I felt his lips kissing my skin and his tongue sucking it. "Please stop!" I cried out, his abuse not only hurt me physically, but started traumatising my mind.

"I just want to leave Xander a little present, soon you will be owned by me."

Then he bit me, just like the monster he is. I screamed out in pain.

He put me down again and just watched.

The only thing I could do was scream and cry out in pain.

He again, smiled his evil smile and left the room, but not before sending me a kiss.

I just sat there, traumatised.

Chapter 11

"Arabelle, it's me." Xander whispered.I just sat in the corner and cried, my whole body shaking in fear. I was absolutely terrified, of not only Evan, but of everything.

Xander tried picking me up, but I shrieked and pushed myself further back at his advances. "Arabelle, what happened? We're all okay, nothing can hurt you anymore?"

I lifted my head and looked him in the eyes. I couldn't help the sobs leaving my mouth.I stood up and fell into his arms, hugging him to death.

"Arabelle, what happened, why is your neck bloody?" He questioned, I answered with another whimper.

He aggressively picked me up, this time succeeding, and carried me out of the room. I could practically feel the anger radiating off him.

I hid my head in his shoulders, too scared to look at my surroundings.

„Lukas, call the Brothers. It's an emergency." Xander yelled.He continued carrying me, until we reached my room and he carefully sat me down.

"Shhhh, it's okay Arabelle" he softly cooed into my ear. "No one can hurt you anymore, Babygirl"I started crying hard."E-evan, h-he" I sobbed, not letting Xander go.His grip on me tightened."What, darling?"

"H-he came a-and b-bit me a-and th-threatened me.H-he s-said I-I would b-be his" I croaked out.

Xander listened silently, I could tell he was drowning in anger. He softly separated my arms from around him and stood up.I curled up in a ball again and watched him from my bed, as he screamed in anger and punched the wall. My desk flew around the room and shattered to pieces, then he stood still.He turned around and looked intimidating as ever. I, however, was not scared of him, he would protect me.

"I'm not ever letting you out of my sight again, we will be attached by the hip Arabelle." He spit out, I nodded slowly.

He watched me with a worried look on his face and then sighed.

"Come on little one, we're going to treat the wound on your neck."I was about to stand up, but instead he picked me up again and carried me to the the attached bathroom.He sat me on the sink and pulled the first aid kit out of one of the cupboards."Come closer, babygirl."He then started looking at my neck. His soft eyes turned angry once again and he lowly whispered to himself "I will kill that motherfucker".

I hugged him again.

After disinfecting the wound, he bandaged my neck.

He put the first aid kit away and was about to leave the bathroom. He then turned around and looked at me expectingly.I jumped off the sink and followed him.

"Arabelle" Someone from beside me said. I shrieked in surprise and fear, still traumatised from the earlier events

Xander growled angrily "Be fucking careful, Lukas"."I'm so sorry Ara, how are you? Are you okay?"I took in his tall form and noticed a relatively big bandage wrapped around his shoulder.

"Oh my god Lukas? You got shot??? Are you okay??? What happened? Please tell me you're okay!" I panicked and tried hugging him, but Xander pulled me into his side. I blushed a little, he was taking the "joined at the hip" thing very seriously.

Lukas giggled "Oh Ara I'm fine, just a graze. Believe me, the other guy got it ten times worse"

I poured at his 'humour' "This is not to be laughed at, Lukas. You could have gotten seriously hurt fighting like that."

"Oh girly, you're adorable. But we're paid to fight. Protecting you is our job."

I frowned a little. I know that. Still, it is difficult to imagine that they could possibly die and it would be my fault.

"Xander, they will be here at 4am, they're taking the jet." Lukas said, I instantly knew who he was talking about.

"Perfect, I'll be downstairs. From now on, Arabelle and I are going to sleep in the same room, tell Roxanne to prepare a bed."

I gasped."What no! Xander I understand the importance, but I can't sleep in the same room as you, you're a man after all" My face turned a bright red colour as I mumbled out the words.

"I'm not familiar with being that close to men." I looked down. Of course I was surrounded by hundreds of men, but they always kept their distance.

We barely ever talked for heaven's sake! And Xander has always been so mean, he was sweet today, but what about tomorrow?

"Arabelle, this concerns your safety. You have absolutely no say in this. Your brothers gave me a job and I will do my best to fulfill the task given. Plus, it's a lot easier to protect you, when I'm close to you and know where you are at all times" I blushed again.

I really did not know what to say anymore, he'd going to be in my room 24/7? Us two? Alone?

„Can Lukas stay with us, please?" I pleaded.

„Yes, 4 eyes are better than 2 after all." Lukas jumped in.

„Absolutely fucking not! Lukas get that idea right out of your fucked up head." Xander growled aggressively.

„Whatever, that's settled then. Arabelle go to the kitchen, you will be dining and then go to bed." Xander ordered.

„Lol wtf, who even are you? Her bodyguard or her daddy?"

„Shut the fuck up Lukas, before I smash your ugly face."

„O-okay, ehem, I'am on my way." I shyly mumbled and made me way to the kitchen.

Ascot, our cook, prepared delicious chicken casserole.The dinner was silent again. Not even Lukas said a single word, Michael kept quiet as usual and Xander was busy glaring at Lukas throughout the entire meal.

A second after I put away my spoon Xander pulled me up by my arm. "We're going to bed."

I looked pleadingly at Michael and Lukas, begging them to say something. They just looked away.

I got pulled up the stairs and into the room.

A few meters away from my bed, stood a second bed. Xander's bed.

Oh boy, this will be fun...

Chapter 12

"So, uhm, Xander?" I mumbled "I, eh, I really want to take a shower""Okay let's go" he said and pulled me towards the bathroom. What was he about to do?

"X-Xander? What are you doing? I don't mean to be rude, but I don't think you're meant to take a shower with a g-girl." I stuttered nervously.

"Arabelle, I told you I'm not letting you out of my sight. I'll always be at your side, doesn't matter if you're in the kitchen, hallway, or even the bathroom." He said sternly.

"B-but..."

"No buts. This concerns your safety. It's my job to protect you and you're only safe with me next to you."

I nodded in understanding. It was weird, sure, but I'd just have to get used to it. I mean, Xander IS here to keep me safe and if he thinks that I'll only be safe with him in the same room, then so be it.

Still...

This is not how I imagined this to be like...

"But please do me a favour and don't look, okay?" I pleaded. Showering with him in the same room was bad enough, but I wouldn't live to see the next morning if he saw me naked.

"Oh Arabelle, I wouldn't even want to look" He answered condescendingly.

"O-oh, okay." I whispered and made my way to the bathroom.

He followed me and stood in front of the bathroom door, he shut it and locked it.

"X-xander?"He seemed annoyed."I'll turn around now, take off your clothes and put them on the chair over there." He gruffly said and pointed at the chair in the corner.

Then he turned around.

Still feeling highly uncomfortable, I started fiddling with my shirt.I slowly pulled it over my head and unsurely stepped out of my trousers.

I slowly opened the hook of my bra, while watching his head. I was praying he didn't suddenly turn around.Instead, I heard a low groan.

"Hurry up already and get into the damn shower." He sounded pained.

"Are you sure you're okay? I mean you can always go to the nurse, you don't have to stay here." I rushed out, incredibly nervous and beet red.

„Just get into the fucking shower, Arabelle."

I squeaked and quickly put my undergarments, shirt and trousers onto the chair, before finally stepping into the shower.

I made sure I had the right temperature, before squirting a bit of the shower gel into my hands. Rose jam by Lush, my favourite.

I hurried up and was finally able to rinse out the conditioner, when the shower bottle suddenly dropped to the floor.

I tried picking it up, but the floor was just super slippery.

Before I could finally reach the little bottle, I lost balance and of course I fell.

A little shriek left my mouth, when suddenly the door was pulled open and a worried Xander looked down at me. Me.As in my body.As in my naked body.Naked.

I started blushing like crazy and tried covering my body a little.

Xander pulled himself away from me and grabbed a towel, put it around me and then picked up my body.

Totally surprised at his actions, I screamed a little.

"X-Xander, I swear I'm okay! Please, please let me down!" I pleaded, incredibly embarrassed.

I mean he saw me naked! I started panicking a little.

However, he did let me down. He sat me onto the bed and carefully examined my leg.

"You're not okay. You sprained your ankle, while pulling that little stunt earlier. Why are you so fucking clumsy." He muttered angrily.

I didn't answer, I just looked down feeling really embarrassed.

"I'm sorry" I whispered, pulled the towel tighter around myself and never looked up from my lap.

Xander just sighed and called someone."Tell Jack to bring up a bandage and a few ice packs. Oh and also tell him to bring some Ibuprofen 600.

The idiot sprained her ankle.-Yeah, you're right. She's way too clumsy for her own good.-Alright, thanks." He ended the phone call.

He came back to where I was sitting and lifted my chin up with two fingers.

He looked into my eyes and then let my chin go.He got two pillows and motioned for me to lay down. I pushed myself up on my elbows, while lying down and observed Xander curiously.

Without saying anything, he grabbed my injured leg and carefully put it on top of the stacked pillows.

Then someone knocked the door and Xander pulled it open.Jack came into the room, looking at me.He was about to hand me the things Xander ordered earlier. But Xander blocked the way.

„Give them to me, Jack." he growled angrily.

„Okay, okay, chill." Jack said and raised both his arms defensively. He here really looked at him though, he kept staring at me.

„And if you don't take your fucking eyes off her, you'll never be able to see anything again, I swear." He threatened.

I cowered at his threat, it scared me. And oh sweet piggy, I would have died on the spot, if the threat had been directed at me.

Jack scurried our of the room and shit it again.

„Xander? Is everything okay?"

„It's not fucking okay for you tho lie there defensively, in only a tiny fucking towel."

Remembering the towel, I turned beet red.

How could I even forget??? Both Xander and Jack saw me in only a towel!!! I grabbed one of my beloved pillows and hid my face in the sweet softness.

While I hid behind my only friend in this room, Xander treated my leg. I didn't dare look at him, way too embarrassed.

But he had other plans. He picked me up and, once again, carried me towards the bathroom.

He sat me down onto the toilet and handed me my toothbrush.

"Wait and don't move, I'll be back in a second." He ran out of the bathroom.

Not even a second passed before he came back and handed me one of his large T-shirts.He then turned around.

"Xander? I also have my own Pyjamas?" I questioned.

"Doesn't matter, just hurry up."

I dropped the towel and pulled the shirt over my head.I proceeded to brush my teeth, washed my face and put a bit of lotion on.

Xander turned around again.

"Ready for bed?" He grumbled

"Yep" I grinned up at him.

He picked me up and carried me to my bed.

He then pulled of his shirt and pushed down his trousers.

Oh holy piggy.

His muscles stretched, as he pulled his shirt off. His abs stood out clearly and the veins on his arms protruded. No wonder he was able to carry me everywhere.

Embarrassed that I pretty much stared at him, I turned around and pulled the blanket over my head.

How was I going to survive from now on?

Chapter 13

X ander

Fuck, fuck, fuck.

I rolled around the small folding bed.I could not get her out of my mind. Her little perfect body.The sweet sweet curves. Beautiful.Fucking beautiful and her beauty was my fucking problem.And now we'd have to sleep in the same damn room. I tried not to watch her sleep, but that turned out to be a lot harder than I initially thought.

I saw her squirming all over her bed, she's been doing that for the past hour or so.I knew she had a nightmare of some kind, probably processing everything that happened to her.I still can't get that bastard out of my head. I can't completely blame him though, it was my fault she got hurt like that.I should have protected her, I should have stayed with her, like I promised her brothers once.

„P-please,n-no." Arabelle whimpered in her sleep.

She used to look so calm while sleeping, now her face is scrunched up and a terrified aura is surrounding her.

Why the fuck did I ever leave her alone?

I slowly approached her bed, trying to control myself and not jump her and kiss the shit out of her, like I always kind of wanted to.

My own feelings disturbed me. I never intended to fall in love with her, that never was my plan and I only realised my feelings very recently.

The little beauty kept squirming around and a few tears rolled down her cheeks.

"Shh, darling. It's okay, it's me." I whispered into her ear and carefully took her into my arms.I shook her a little, in order to wake her up.

"Shh, baby girl, wake up." Her eyes fluttered.

"X-xander?" She whimperd, her eyes red and her cheeks wet.

"Calm down, it's okay now." She tried pulling away.

"X-Xander w-what are you doing in my bed?" I pulled her back into my arms and held her tightly.

"Don't be stubborn, you were crying in your sleep and I'm making sure you're safe."

"I-I really don't know about this." She muttered quietly. Her face was a bright red, her blush even reached down her neck. It was obvious, she wasn't exactly resisting, she was just so fucking shy.

Respecting her embarrassment, I let her go. She instantly started shuddering at the coldness of the room.

It really was freezing outside, but I knew of her habit of always opening the window during the night, so I didn't protest.

She cuddled into her blanket, looking like a little cute worm.Adorable.

"What was your dream about?"

"Ehm, I forgot?" She said hesitantly.

"Arabelle, you better tell me now, or help me god." I growled. My anger wasn't even directed at her, but thinking about what that dick did to her, I couldn't control myself.

She flinched back, seemingly scared of the tone I used.

God damn, be fucking careful Xander. She's fragile at the moment. My conscience reminded me.

"I'm not angry at you, Arabelle. I know you dreamt of him, I'm angry at him for even having had the opportunity to look at you."

She blushed again. "Thank you Xander, for always being here for me."

"Don't worry, that's my job."

Her expression saddened.

Fuck

"Oh..., still, thank you" she smiled at me, a beautiful smile.

I actually tried smiling back at her, I'm sure it looked terrific. Smiling wasn't the norm for me and I therefor didn't do it a lot, but for her I'd cute my fucking dick off, although I'm sure she'd miss it. I smirked at my own thought.

"Are you okay? Xander?" Arabelle looked up at me, with her cute innocent eyes.

Good thing she doesn't know what I'm thinking about.

"Let's go to bed now." I laid down beside her. Her bed was huge anyway.

"What are you doing Xander? You can't sleep with me?" She yelled.

"Darling, I'm not sleeping with you, I'm sleeping next to you. I'm sure you'd know the difference, if I were to show you."

She looked confused at first, then her face scrunched up in disgust, then she started blushing like crazy.

"Stop with those jokes." The cutie mumbled.

"But Arabelle, you know you wouldn't have any more nightmares with me next to you. We both know that, so just let me protect you."I spoke in a calm, serious tone. I was actually doing her a favour, her sleep would kill mine. It already took enough control, to just be in the same room with her, but the same bed?

Fuck me.

Quite literally.

Shit, I sounded like a desperate teenage girl, who just watched Robert Psomething in Twilight.

She didn't answer, she just shifted to the side, making the gap between us as big as possible.

I rolled my eyes at her behaviour.

"I'm not gonna attack you anyway. No need to worry about that."

"Oh, okay then." Her cheeks turned red, once again, as she came a little closer.

And as I expected, it didn't even take her ten minutes to fall asleep again.

I, however, was a different story.

I couldn't get over the close proximity. Shit. What was I thinking?

Her breathing picked up, she started squirming around again. Another nightmare?

I pulled her into my arms, knowing I could stop her nightmares. She instantly calmed down.

————————————————

Sorry guys, this was kinda cringey lol, but don't we love some good cringe?

Chapter 14

I cuddled more into the warm chest that laid underneath me.Wait, this definitely does not feel like a pillow.I slowly opened my eye and screeched back at the sight. A half naked Xander laid underneath me, one arm still kinda wrapped around my waist.I tried prying his fingers off my body, just to get some distance between us.His bipolar behaviour confused me.What was going on with him? A few weeks ago he wouldn't come near me even if his life depended on it.But now? I'm practically caged in his arms.

Just as I thought about being caged, he tightened his grip.

"What are you doing?" He grumbled tiredly."P-Please let me go" As if he just realised our position, he shoved me away from him.I pouted."This is my bed, the only one who will do the shoving is me." I stated proudly, he just huffed.

I ignored his strange attitude, stood up and hurried to the bathroom to get ready.I heard some rumbling from my room, so I assumed he got ready for the day as well.

Once I finished my business, I left the bathroom, just to discover that he was already waiting at the door.

Normally he would comment on anything, but now he kept quiet. What provoked the change?

"Are you okay?" I asked shyly. Was it even my business?

"Why are you asking?"He said in his dark voice.

"You seem very different lately. I don't know. Less angry?" I rambled on.

"Oh, that. Nothing happened, now stop being so inquisitive and go to the kitchen."He grumbled.

Instead of asking further questions I ran down the stairs, straight to the kitchen.To my surprise Lukas stood at the stove, making some pancakes. "Lukas!" I squealed and ran towards him."Babe, there you finally are. Romeo over here was waiting for his Juliet." He joked around in a flirtatious way, which made me blush.

"Shut up, Andersson" The man behind me growled angrily.

"Get away from that asshole Arabelle, you can help me set the table for the both of us." Lukas said and pulled me even closer to him.I freed myself and started setting the table.

"I really fucking hate you, Andersson. You better be careful." Xander said darkly.

"Well that love is not one-sided, Black. Keep your hands to yourself though, I'm better off with 'Belly over here."I couldn't hold back the giggle as I heard the way he called me.Bad move though, Xander clenched his fists even harder.

"Calm down around my sister." A voice suddenly interrupted.

"Derek?" I shouted excitedly and ran into his arms. "I missed you, little one." He said warmly and hugged me back. "Where are the other two?" I looked up to him.

"Well, we're coming separately. We weren't together when..." He looked down angrily. "Oh yeah, hm, so when will the be arriving?" "Probably within the next two hours, I" He got interrupted by my grumbling tummy.

"Oh little one, I forgot that I disturbed your meal. Lukas come and serve her some of those damn pancakes. Xander, get her some cutlery, a plate and the bottle of syrup." Both grumbled, but complied nonetheless.

"Are you sure you're alright?" Derek whispered in my ear worriedly.

"Hm yeah, just a little shaken up still." I whispered back, but much quieter.

" Babygirl, here are some delicious pancakes, for the princess." Lukas stated and was about to serve me some of the mouth watering preciousness, but was interrupted by a loud bang.

Xander dropped the syrup and glared at us. As I saw the glare directed at me, I shrunk back into my chair.

Derek watched the scene play out and pulled me towards him, seemingly protecting me from the two strange men.

"Lukas, you're going to take over Xander's position as Arabelle's personal guard." He calmly stated.

Then all hell broke loose.

"WHAT?" Xander screamed. He threw a chair over and puffed angrily.

"You see Xander, you need to figure out your temperament first. Calm down, I thought about this for some time now."

"I'm the only one who will ever be able to properly protect Arabelle, you know that." Xander tried defending himself, trying to calm himself down.

"When it does come down to it, you might be. But are you also to protect Arabelle from yourself?"

And that's the last thing I headed, before Lukas pulled me out of the kitchen, straight the rose garden.

www.ingramcontent.com/pod-product-compliance
Lightning Source LLC
Chambersburg PA
CBHW071357200726
48294CB00004B/1198